(A)

This book belongs to

For Stanley Becker

First published in Great Britain in 1993 by Andersen Press Ltd., 20 Vauxhall Bridge Road, London SW1V 2SA. This
paperback edition first published in 1998 by Andersen Press Ltd.Published in Australia by Random House
Australia Pty., 20 Alfred Street, Milsons Point, Sydney, NSW 2061. All rights reserved. Colour separated in
Switzerland by Photolitho AG, Gossau, Zürich. Printed and bound in Italy by Grafiche AZ, Verona.

10   9   8   7   6   5   4   3   2   1

British Library Cataloguing in Publication Data available.

ISBN 0 86264 488 7

This book has been printed on acid-free paper

Dottie

Written and illustrated by
Peta Coplans

Andersen Press · London

Dottie was always growing things. It drove her parents crazy.
She started in the garden.
"Not in the GARDEN!" said Dad.
"Gardens are for burying bones and rolling in the grass."

She grew things in the house.
"Not in the HOUSE, Dottie!" said Mum.
"Look at this muddy carpet!"

"Dogs don't grow things," said Mum and Dad together.
"Who says?" asked Dottie.
"EVERYONE!" said Mum and Dad.
"Now be a good dog. Go out and chase a postman, instead."

Dottie went to visit Duck.
He was putting on his rollerskates.
"Ducks don't rollerskate!" said Dottie.

"Don't they?" said Duck.

"I do."

On the way to Rabbit's house, Dottie saw Cat.

"What are you doing?" said Dottie. "Cats don't like water."

"Don't they?" said Cat.

"I do."

Rabbit was mixing colours when Dottie arrived.

"You can't do that!" said Dottie. "Rabbits don't paint pictures."

"Don't they?" said Rabbit. "I do."

Dottie went home. She knew what she was going to do.

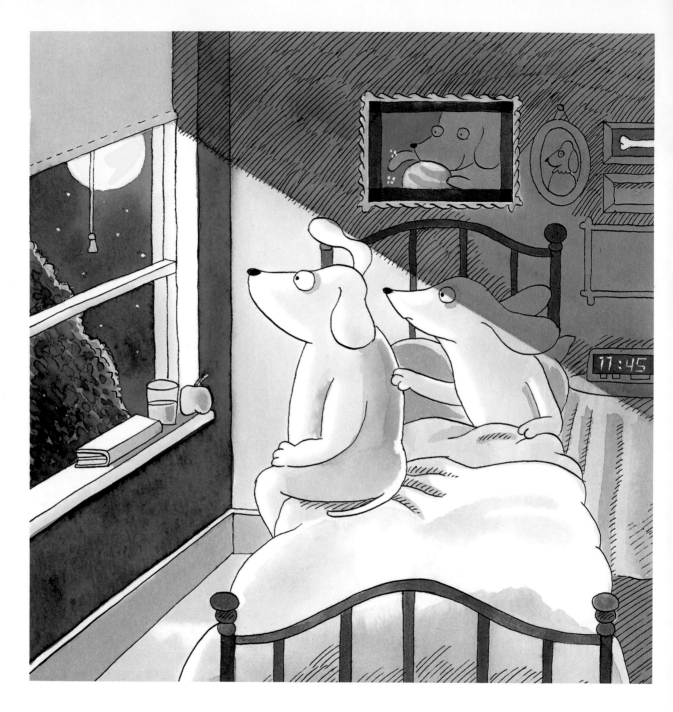

A few nights later, Dad sat up in bed. He woke Mum.
"Listen!" he said. "I hear strange noises outside."

"It could be a burglar!" said Mum.
They sneaked downstairs.

In the furthest corner of the garden, they found the answer.
"It's me," said Dottie. "I'm growing things."
"Go to bed IMMEDIATELY!" said Dad.
"This MINUTE!" said Mum.
"And no more growing things," they said together.
"Dogs don't grow things!"
Dottie went to bed, but Mum and Dad couldn't sleep.

"Why can't she be like other dogs?" Dad sighed.
"She IS very good at growing things," said Mum.
"Couldn't she have a few little plants? I saw strawberries."
"I LOVE fresh strawberries!" said Dad.
"And lettuce," said Mum. "And lovely runner beans!"
"Go to sleep!" said Dad. "You're making me hungry!"

It was Dottie's birthday a few weeks later.
Rabbit, Cat and Duck were all invited to her party.
After cake and lemonade, Dottie took her friends outside.

"Look!" she said. "It's from Mum and Dad."
"That's a big present," said Cat. "What is it?"
"Open it!" shouted Rabbit. "Let's see what's inside!"

"A watering can!" said Cat. "You don't need THAT!"
"Or flower pots, or seeds, OR a rake!" said Duck.
"EVERYONE knows dogs don't grow things," said Rabbit.

"Don't they?" said Mum.
"Don't they?" said Dad.

"Don't they?" said Dottie. "I do!"

THE
END

More Andersen Press paperback picture books!